IMAGINE THAT

Licensed exclusively to Imagine That Publishing Ltd
Tide Mill Way, Woodbridge, Suffolk, IP12 1AP, UK
www.imaginethat.com
Copyright © 2019 Imagine That Group Ltd
All rights reserved
0 2 4 6 8 9 7 5 3 1
Manufactured in China

Retold by Joshua George
Illustrated by Kimberley Barnes

ISBN 978-1-78958-198-0

A catalogue record for this book is available from the British Library

The Little Mermaid

Hans Christian Andersen

Retold by Joshua George
Illustrated by Kimberley Barnes

Deep in the ocean, where the water is as blue as a cornflower and as clear as crystal, is the Sea King's castle.

Of the Sea King's six daughters, the youngest was the most beautiful, and had the loveliest singing voice.

The little mermaid loved two things: singing, and listening to stories about the world above the sea.

'When you are fifteen,' said her grandmother, 'you may swim up to the surface. Then you will see the world above the sea.'

On the little mermaid's fifteenth birthday, she swam up to the surface as lightly as a bubble, excited about all the things she might see.

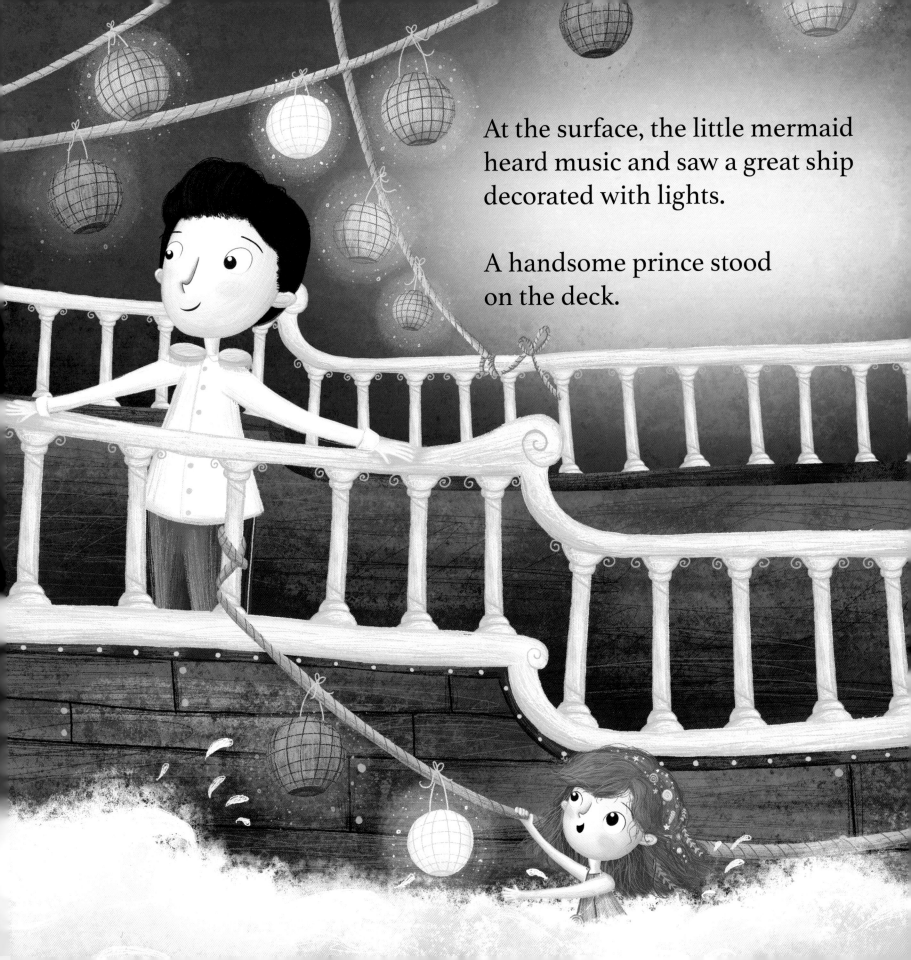

At the surface, the little mermaid heard music and saw a great ship decorated with lights.

A handsome prince stood on the deck.

As the little mermaid watched, a great storm approached and the calm water turned into huge waves. The waves broke the ship in two and it began to sink!

'I must save the prince!' thought the little mermaid, searching among the wreckage.

Once she had finally found him, she carefully held his head above the water and let the waves carry them to dry land.

When the prince began to wake, the little mermaid slipped away into the water.

From that day on, the little mermaid spent many nights watching the palace from close to the shore.

She wished more than anything that she had legs instead of a tail.

'Perhaps the sea witch could help me,' she wondered. 'I will go and ask her.'

'I can make a potion that will turn your tail into legs,' said the sea witch, 'but if the prince does not marry you, your legs will turn back into a tail again.'

'And my price,' cackled the witch, 'is your beautiful voice for every day you are on land!'

'I agree,' said the little mermaid quietly.

That night, the little mermaid drank the potion. When she woke the prince was standing in front of her ... and her tail had turned into a pair of legs!

But when the little mermaid opened her mouth to talk, she could not speak a single word.

The royal family treated the little mermaid kindly and even gave her a room in the palace, although without her voice she could not thank them.

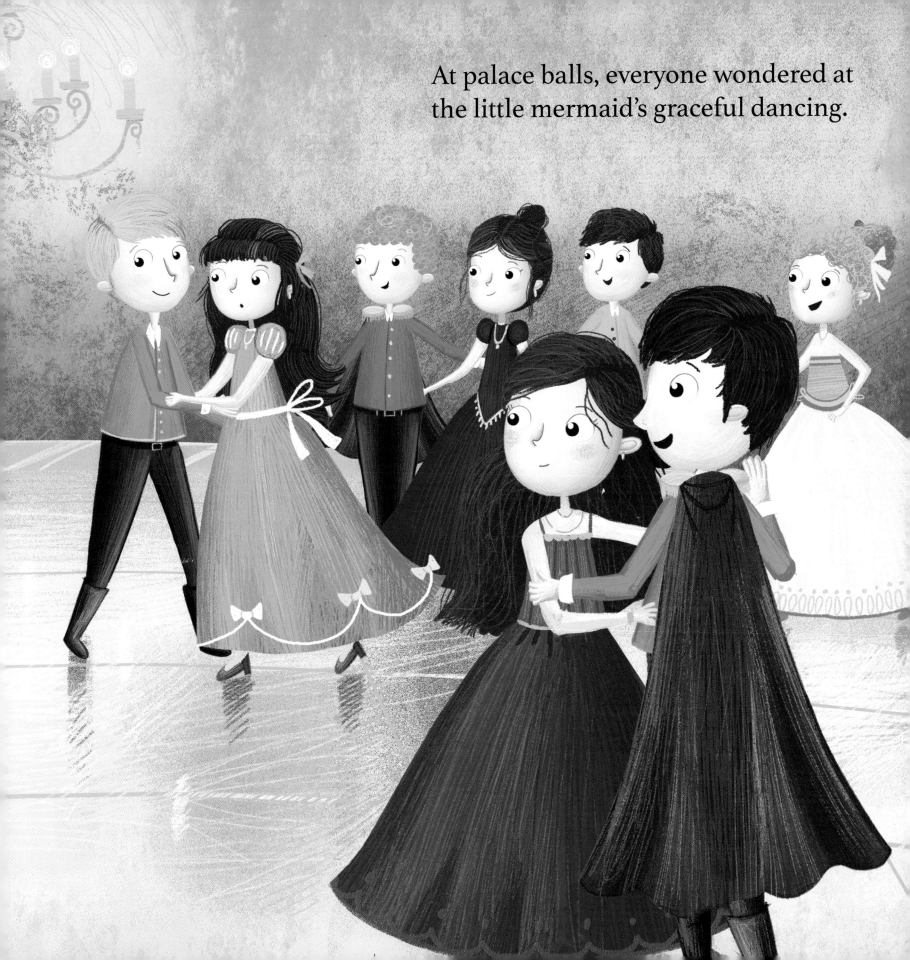

At palace balls, everyone wondered at the little mermaid's graceful dancing.

The prince and the little mermaid spent many happy days exploring the kingdom together.

The little mermaid loved the prince, but she could not tell him how she felt.

'You are like the sister I never had,' the prince laughed.

The following spring, the prince took the little mermaid on a trip to a faraway country. 'My father is sending me to meet a princess,' he explained.

'If only I could tell him that I am a princess,' thought the little mermaid sadly.

When they arrived, the prince fell in love with the princess and they agreed to marry.

On the night of the wedding
there was a party on the
king's finest ship.

There was food, fireworks,
music and dancing.
The little mermaid danced
more gracefully than ever.

The next morning, the little mermaid was nowhere to be found.

The prince never saw the little mermaid again. But for years after, he thought he heard a beautiful song drift up from the water below and saw the splash of a shimmering tail.